Bill's Silly Hat

by Susan Gates

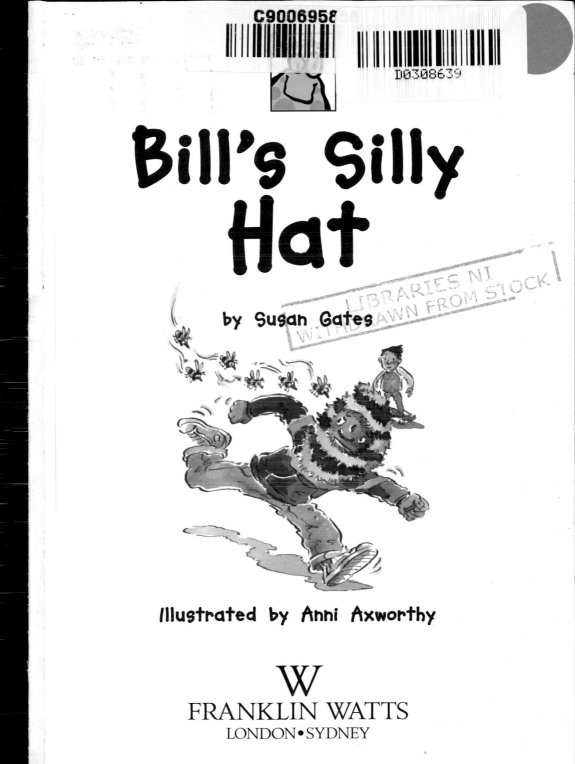

Illustrated by Anni Axworthy

W
FRANKLIN WATTS
LONDON•SYDNEY

First published in 2013 by
Franklin Watts
338 Euston Road
London
NW1 3BH

Franklin Watts Australia
Level 17/207 Kent Street
Sydney
NSW 2000

A CIP catalogue record for this book is available
from the British Library.

ISBN 978 1 4451 1611 2 (hbk)
ISBN 978 1 4451 1617 4 (pbk)

Series Editor: Jackie Hamley
Series Advisor: Catherine Glavina
Series Designer: Peter Scoulding

Printed in China

Franklin Watts is a divison of
Hachette Children's Books,
an Hachette UK company.
www.hachette.co.uk

"I don't like this hat Gran
made me," said Bill.
"It's silly!"

"You have to wear it,"
said Mum, "or Gran
will be very upset."

"It makes me look like a bee!" said Bill.

Bill had to go out in the hat.

He went to the park.

A big boy shouted,

"Hey! Bumble Bee Boy!"

Another boy grinned, "Buzz!" Bill said, "I'm taking this hat off! Everyone's laughing at me!"

Then Bill thought, "Oh no!
Is that Gran over there?"
Bill put the hat back on.

But it was the wrong
way round!
"I can't see!" Bill cried.

Bill just missed
the pond.

He stumbled through
the skate park.

Then he fell into the
sandpit.

Bill got out. He put his hat on the right way round.

"Oh no!" said Bill. "Now bees are after me! They think I'm a Queen Bee!"

Bill ran as fast as he could!
"Good! They've gone!"
he said.

Bill walked home.
"I have to get rid of
this silly hat somehow,"
he said to himself.

At home, Bill's little sister was sad. "I don't know any songs for the talent contest," she cried.

Bill had an idea. "I'll teach you a song," he said.

Buzzy Bee! Buzzy Bee!
Buzz if you like,
but don't sting ME!

"What's that dance she's doing?" asked Gran.

"It's a bee dance,
of course," said Bill.

"She won the contest!"
cried Bill's mum.

"Thanks, Bill!" said Dad.
"You helped her win."

Bill's little sister said,
"I love this bee hat!"

"Keep it. It's yours!"
said Bill.

"Wow!" said Bill's little sister. "Are you sure? Bill, you are the best brother!"

"I'm glad SOMEONE likes that hat," thought Bill.

Puzzle 1

Put these pictures in the correct order.
Now tell the story in your own words.
How short can you make the story?

happy   pleased

embarrassed

kind   mean

understanding

Choose the words which best describe each character. Can you think of any more? Pretend to be one of the characters!

Answers

Puzzle 1

The correct order is:

1b, 2e, 3a, 4d, 5f, 6c

Puzzle 2

Bill The correct word is embarrassed.

The incorrect words are happy, pleased.

Boy The correct word is mean.

The incorrect words are kind, understanding.

Look out for more Leapfrog stories:

Mary and the Fairy
ISBN 978 0 7496 9142 4

Pippa and Poppa
ISBN 978 0 7496 9140 0

The Bossy Cockerel
ISBN 978 0 7496 9141 7

The Best Snowman
ISBN 978 0 7496 9143 1

Big Bad Blob
ISBN 978 0 7496 7796 1

Cara's Breakfast
ISBN 978 0 7496 7797 8

Sticky Vickie
ISBN 978 0 7496 7986 6

Handyman Doug
ISBN 978 0 7496 7987 3

The Wrong House
ISBN 978 0 7496 9480 7

Prickly Ballroom
ISBN 978 0 7496 9475 3

That Noise!
ISBN 978 0 7496 9479 1

The Scary Chef's Scarecrow
ISBN 978 0 7496 9476 0

Alex and the Troll
ISBN 978 0 7496 9478 4

The Frog Prince and the Kitten
ISBN 978 1 4451 1614 3*
ISBN 978 1 4451 1620 4

The Animals' Football Cup
ISBN 978 0 7496 9477 7

The Animals' Football Camp
ISBN 978 1 4451 1610 5*
ISBN 978 1 4451 1616 7

Bill's Bouncy Shoes
ISBN 978 0 7496 7990 3

Bill's Scary Backpack
ISBN 978 0 7496 9468 5

Bill's Silly Hat
ISBN 978 1 4451 1611 2*
ISBN 978 1 4451 1617 4

Little Joe's Balloon Race
ISBN 978 0 7496 7989 7

Little Joe's Boat Race
ISBN 978 0 7496 9467 8

Little Joe's Horse Race
ISBN 978 1 4451 1613 6*
ISBN 978 1 4451 1619 8

Felix and the Kitten
ISBN 978 0 7496 7988 0

Felix Takes the Blame
ISBN 978 0 7496 9466 1

Felix, Puss in Boots
ISBN 978 1 4451 1615 0*
ISBN 978 1 4451 1621 1

Cheeky Monkey on Holiday
ISBN 978 0 7496 7991 0

Cheeky Monkey's Treasure Hunt
ISBN 978 0 7496 9465 4

Cheeky Monkey's Big Race
ISBN 978 1 4451 1612 9*
ISBN 978 1 4451 1618 1

For details of all our titles go to: www.franklinwatts.co.uk

*hardback

Bill's Silly Hat

Bill hates the hat
his gran has knitted for him.
It makes him look like a bee!
He must wear it or she will be
upset. Can he get rid of it?

Series Advisor: Catherine Glavina,
Senior Teaching Fellow, Institute of Education,
University of Warwick.

If you liked reading this, why not try another *Leapfrog* story?

**Find more stories
and reading tips at**
www.**its fun to read**.co.uk

£4.99

FRANKLIN WATTS

ISBN 978-1-4451-1617-4

9 781445 116174

www.franklinwatts.co.uk